Alfred Austin

The Season

A Satire

Alfred Austin

The Season
A Satire

ISBN/EAN: 9783337146863

Printed in Europe, USA, Canada, Australia, Japan

Cover: Foto ©Andreas Hilbeck / pixelio.de

More available books at **www.hansebooks.com**

"Muse,
...... draped discreetly in a skirt and vest,
Which just withhold the secrets they suggest."

THE SEASON:

A SATIRE.

BY

ALFRED AUSTIN.

WITH FRONTISPIECE OF "THE MODERN MUSE," BY

THOMAS GEORGE COOPER.

Slender.—Why do your dogs bark so? be there bears i' th' Town?

Anne Page.—I think there are, Sir! I heard them talked of.

Slender.—I love the sport well; . . . but the women have so cried and shrieked at it, that it passed.

Merry Wives of Windsor.

LONDON:
ROBERT HARDWICKE, 192, PICCADILLY.

1861.

"The diseases of society can, no more than corporal maladies, be prevented or cured without being spoken about in plain language."—JOHN STUART MILL, *"Principles of Political Economy."*

THE SEASON.

I SING the Season.   Muse! whose sway extends

Where Hyde begins beyond where Tyburn ends:

Muse! not like vulgar Muses, known and nude,

Who look the trollop yet who act the prude,

But draped discreetly in a skirt and vest

Which just withhold the secrets they suggest:

Muse, at whose toilet (sure the sweetest shrine)

Rimmel presents his last " pommade divine :"

Mistress avowed where'er Man's lofty brain

Invents a colour or conceals a stain :

Muse, earth-begot! equipped from hip to heel

In loose array of penetrable steel :

Fashion yclept! without whose granted spell
No critic praises and no verses sell,
Accept my couplets; make my strains select,
Parade each beauty, powder each defect;
So that my lines, quick, sparkling as your eyes,
Storm the Town's Circles with a swift surprise!

   Why sing the Season? cautious critics say:
Why write a Satire? only Epics pay.
The world grows earnest, and no more endures
A dilettante flippant pen like yours.
Sing of the Zodiac! the Creator's Mind!
The past—the future—Mansions of Mankind!
The secret Spheres of blessedness or woe!
Sing all, sing any—save the one you know.
Shriek—start—pant—palpitate—pause—prove to
     men
There is some splendid purpose in your pen.

Convert your cut-throats, leave your Phrynes
    chaste;

Flaunt moral diamonds (who will know they're
    paste?) :

Compete with Meredith :[a] discreetly steal

Your plot, your apophthegms, and top "Lucile!"

---

[a] This clever but somewhat spasmodic young man, who
is too modest to write under his patronymic, is, perhaps, too
modest likewise to have his own opinions. But if he will
not adopt the *name*, to which he has a right, why does he
adopt and dress up again for the public, already tolerably
well acquainted with them, the *dicta* of his father, to
which he has none? If, however, he considers the family
novels free warren for him, what excuse can he have for
poaching on the plot of "Sword and Gown?" Has he
piscary and turbary over Mr. Lawrence's preserves? If
he have, he has exercised his right unsparingly.

I would point out to him, that in one serious particular
he has overlooked parental admonition. In one of those
charming conversations, prefixed to each Book of "My
Novel," Pisistratus Caxton combats the idea of his rela-
tions, that he can make the personages of his story act
and talk just as it pleases him. He urges with admirable
force that, once started on a certain path, the author has

Spawn bastard spondees spuriously Greek,

With modern tawdry drape the grand Antique,

Olympus vulgarize with clumsy care—

Cambridge rewarded Kingsley ^b with a Chair.

---

no control over the destination of his characters. They
must be dramatically consistent with themselves. Goethe
means the same thing when he says, "A man's history is
his character." Had Owen Meredith even a glimpse of this
truth, we should have been spared the final tableau of
repentance and forgiveness which concludes "Lucile."
Really, men and women—men certainly—are not in the
habit of repenting in the ridiculously promiscuous manner
attributed to them from, I suppose, some preconceived
notions of morality. Why may not a few at least be
allowed to remain in ideal histories, as most, who have
ever been, remain in real life, wicked to the last?

^b "Andromeda and other Poems" has attained to the
honours of a second edition. Clergymen seem to be
privileged. Even had we boys—*nous autres*—written and
published

  "As long as lips grow ripe to kiss," &c.
and

 "Kiss me but once and I go. Then raising her neck
  like a sea-bird

Or write blank verse : it moveth more severe :

Moral your metre, if your views be queer ;

And hint, from 'neath a philosophic hood,

The " Social Evil " 's for the social good.

Throw in some politics, some art, and see

What are your chances 'gainst " Aurora ᶜ Leigh."

"Peering up over the wave, from the foam-white swells
of her bosom
" Blushing, she kissed him :"

not even the plea of our "hot youth" and irresponsible
position would have saved us from the denunciations of
the orthodox : but a "saint in crape" who, if lucky, may
become a "saint in lawn," advertises these erotic
effusions side by side with "Good News from God,"
and is not only pardoned but applauded, and not only
applauded but recompensed. The Chair of Modern History at Cambridge is occupied by this reverend rhymester.

ᶜ Will Mrs. Barrett Browning pardon me for saying
that I entertain for her genius great admiration? She is
the only English Poetess who can be justified by Mr. John
Stuart Mill's ordeal. In his dissertation on Alfred
de Vigny, he says :
"The gems alone of thought and fancy are worth setting

These are the bards; for these Apollo's chair,

His bays for these, and none but these shall wear.

    Thanks, thanks, my friends! but all the world

        can give

I care to take, is—liberty to live.

---

with the finished and elaborate workmanship of verse;
and even of them, only those whose effect is heightened
by it."

But its many gems of thought and fancy, and compli-
mentary criticisms thereon despite, "Aurora Leigh" is not
—and no one could make it—a Poem. Her "Poems before
Congress" have been roughly handled. I will not praise
them; but I will assure her that her opinions, not her
versification (both heterodox enough, doubtless), were the
front of her offending. She is living in Italy: and so she
will perhaps be willing to learn, from one still in England,
that silly stanzas have a chance of gaining favour, but
heretical politics not even a hearing. Englishmen are
not altered since Burke wrote in his "Vindication of
Natural Society:"

"A man is allowed sufficient freedom of thought, pro-
vided he knows how to choose his subject properly. You
may criticise freely upon the Chinese constitution, and

Frankly: I want nor chaplet, chair, nor crown,

But only leave to dawdle through the Town ;

Pass where wit flags, delay where it abounds—

Here, take my arm, and let us go the rounds.

One word, my comrade! Let this point be
    clear :

Know that I never condescend to sneer.

He who unwisely, be he man or boy,

Begins to scoff, soon ceases to enjoy.

See wanton bees their senseless mischief rue :

They leave their sting, but oft their bowels too.

Who part with these survive but ill the strife :

Compassion is a requisite of Life.

---

observe with as much severity as you please upon the
absurd tricks or destructive bigotry of the Bonzees. But
the scene is changed as you come homeward, and atheism
or treason may be the name given in Britain to what
would be reason and truth, if asserted of China."

I am no cynic saturate with spleen,

Existence eyeing through a film of green,

To all offensive and whom all offend,

No surly censor, but a frolic friend.

Where is the laugh?   At him—at you—at
    me :

Each meets disaster; all should share the glee.

Fool! to stand crying o'er your broken delf!

The laugh will lessen if you laugh yourself.

I rail at Fashion, prate of Folly, but

This sleeve capacious is the newest cut.

Say you, when Bolus comes to cure your
    sneeze,

" Physician! look you at your own disease ? "

Bennett's *my* Gibus, Houbigant's my glove—

Yet, let me lash the follies that I love.

A scourge so silken need evoke no spleen ;

We laugh the more, unless the joke be seen.

Returning shadows now divide the street:

Free now the Mall from all but Party heat:

Gone the broad glare, save where with borrowed
 bays

Some female Phaeton sets the Drive a-
 blaze;

Or, more defiant, spurning frown and foe,

With slackened rein swift Skittles[d] rules the
 Row.

Though scowling matrons champing steeds restrain,

She flaunts Propriety with flapping mane.

---

[d] Social celebrity travels slowly. Hence, fair readers
who reside wholly in the Provinces may be puzzled by
this passage; but to their Sisters of the Season, Skittles is
as well known and as much an object of interest as the
last shape of Madame Elise; and the skill with which
in talk *à deux* they manœuvre the conversation into
speculations upon her origin, abode, and doings, fully sup-
ports their reputation for tact.

Dear fledgeling damsels! come from country
    nest

To nibble, chirp, and flutter in the West,

Whose clear fresh faces, with their fickle frown

And favour, start like Spring upon the Town:

Less dear, for damaged, damsels! doomed to
    wait,

Whose third—fourth?—season makes half des-
    perate,

Welling with warmth, less potent hour by hour

(As magnets heated lose attractive power):

Or you! nor dear nor damsels, tough and
    tart,

Unmarketable maidens of the mart,

Who, plumpness gone, fine delicacy feint,

And hide your sins in piety and paint;

Or, changing tactics, propped-up bosoms bare

To catch some boyish buyer unaware:

Answer me, all! belle, heiress, flirt, and prue![e]

Who has our notice?   Skittles more or you?

"The nasty wretch! regard her saucy leer!"

Well, own her conquest, and I'll own it queer.

Withal, *not* queer. . .   I am, I must insist,

A most uncompromising moralist.

Wit, frankness, beauty, natural quests of Man,

Provoke his instincts since the world began:

His fine keen scent, evading social skill

To hedge him out, is sure to trespass still.

----

[e] A friendly critic (but are not *all* critics friendly?) asks me what I mean by "prue:" and on my answering "prude," tells me (truly enough) that he has been reading English ever since he was seventeen, and that he has never come across the word.   Many (improvements, as I think, but at any rate) alterations have been made at his generous and enlightened suggestion: but I hold by "prue," and appeal to the women and Ben Jonson. (Who will tell me exactly where?)

No barn-door game, by fluttering mothers reared,

Cooped up from dangers genuine or feared,

Whose wings are clipped to fortify control,

Afford the sport that satisfies the soul.

Is it a marvel, Man's more liberal mood

Should beat the wilds where Nature rears her brood,

Along forbidden border forests roam,

Seeking the breeze he cannot find at home?

Go, girls! to Church! believing all you hear,

Think that their lack of virtue makes them dear;

And heed not me who say that ban and bar

Make you the stupid stunted things you are;

That both would dearer, happier, better be,

Had they your virtue, you their liberty.

But since restraint is privilege from blame,

And loss of fetters is a loss of fame,

Preferring freedom, these forego respect;

Repute *your* choice, you smart beneath neglect.

Alternative ordained by Moral Plan—
To sulk, a doll, or smile, a courtesan !

Incongruous group, they come : the judge's
    hack
With knees as broken as its rider's back :
The counsel's courser stumbling through the
    throng
With wind e'en shorter than its lord's is long :
The statesman's versatile but cautious cob,
That, like its master, sometimes stoops to job :
The foreign Marquis's accomplished colt
Sharing its owner's tendency to bolt :
The—nay enough ; let Cowper's[f] care attest
The worth and vast importance of the rest.

-----

[f] Henry Cowper, First Commissioner of Public Works.

Rise, Britons! rise! ye patriot vestries! call

For monster meetings in St. Martin's Hall!

James, to the rescue!   Shall the Board of
          Works

Treat sons of Hampden like Malays or Turks?

Pym! Magna Charta! Bill of Rights! Bow-
          wow!

You won our liberties : preserve them now!

Heavens! what a hubbub doth the Town divide!

A Revolution? no, a lengthened Ride.

Oh, spare the spot where timid maidens hie

A string to loosen or a swain to tie,

And, favoured by the shy secretive shade,

Prompt the proposal dalliance delayed :

Where tear-dewed lids, choked utterance, sobs
          suppressed,

Coax the confession from a dawdler's breast;

Whence'they, who vainly haunted rout and ride,
Emerge triumphant by a Suitor's side.

Come, let us back, and whilst the Park's alive,
Lean o'er the railings and inspect the Drive.
Look ! as we turn, most loved of all her Line,
If not by Right, by deeds at least divine,
By Nature's self equipped for kind command,
Onward she comes, the Lady of the Land !
Long may each zone its wealth profusely pour
Upon her laplike, peace-protected shore !
Long may the strain come swelling from the
    ships,
Which keeps Victoria on a Nation's lips !
Long, long in thousand eyes that smile be
    seen
Which thinks her woman, though it hails her
    Queen :

Queen, wife, or mother, perfect in each part,

And throned securely in a People's heart !

Still sweeps the long procession, whose array

Gives to the lounger's gaze, as dips the Day,

Its rich reclining and reposeful forms,[g]

Still as bright sunsets after mists or storms,

Who sit and smile, (their morning wranglings

     o'er,

Or dragged and dawdled through one dull day

     more,)

----

[g] An intelligent Peruvian, whom I once took into
Hyde Park, expressed himself much shocked at the
indolent attitudes of our maids and matrons *sans
reproche*: yet he was a descendant of the very people
whose shameless customs Locke, in his "Essay on the
Human Understanding," quoting from Garcilaso de la
Vega, adduces, in order to prove that there are "no innate
practical principles." The indignant criticism of the
descendant of the Tououpinambos would seem to fortify
Locke's theory, though by a retaliatory instance.

As though the life of widow, wife, and girl

Were one long lapsing and voluptuous whirl.

O poor pretence! what eyes so blind but see

The sad, however elegant, ennui?

Think you that blazoned panel, prancing pair,

Befool our vision to the weight they bear!

The richest ribbon, best-lined parasol,

Screen not the woman, though they deck the doll.

The padded corsage and the well-matched hair,

Judicious jupon spreading out the spare,

Sleeves well designed false plumpness to impart,

Leave vacant still the hollows of the heart.

Is not our Lesbia lovely? In her soul,

Lesbia is troubled : Lesbia hath a mole :

And all the splendour of that matchless neck

Consoles not Lesbia for its single speck.

Kate comes from Paris, and a wardrobe brings,

To which poor Edith's are " such common things."

Her pet lace shawl has grown not fit to wear,
And ruined Edith dresses in despair.

   I fear there are who think my satire blind
To all defects except the softer kind.
Says saucy Maud : " You leave the *men* alone :
Is it because their meanness is your own ? "
Perhaps.   But tell me : will you drop a hint
About your sisters I may seize and print ?
Would you to me the mysteries disclose
Of Sophie's boudoir, diary of Rose,
Or—ha ! you start !—your own arcana tell,
Gods ! how my verses would surprise and sell !
But no : whilst men alarmedly declare
" He hits too hard—it really is not fair "—
You, they think hit, are laughing in your sleeves :
" He thinks he *knows*."   Well—honour among
      thieves.

So, though I own that even men have specks,

Like you, I spare the secrets of my sex.

And then, who sees—our eyes not thus designed—

His own base parts of body or of mind?

Though, chance, 'twere well if all, however loth,

Caught now and then a passing glimpse of both.

Still, by severe induction may we guess,

If yours are great, our faults will scarce be less.

Besides: as Sex,[h] in embryotic state,

Is always female till a certain date,

---

[h] This is a fact which the investigations of recent embryologists have made sufficiently certain. In the method of producing males, or sterile females, from the larvæ of bees, may be recognized an analogous if not an exactly similar occurrence. For a short but intelligible account, the reader may consult that popular work, the "Vestiges of Creation."

So are our manly virtues, be assured,

But female vices only more matured;

And just as they, who, armed with lens and knife,

Seek in our frames the principle of life,

Find that the fœtus best assists their aim,

So have *I* found—*my* method is the same.

We best shall learn from fœtal forms; besides,

'Gainst forms developed Decency decides.

Our Figleaf Age shrinks, cognizant of blame,

From honest Manhood with a sickly shame;

Though the whole difference moralists admire

Is—Men but do what women all desire.

   You doubt it?   Why, this moment, see a sign.

All go: but these to dress, whilst those to dine.

Divergence, think you?   Be not duped: their
      aim,

In seeming diverse, is in substance same.

They each require and ply their sensual sport;
The one for praise, the others hunt for port.
And all must own that neither act their best
Till the half-drunk lean over the half-dressed.

    O blesséd moment! . . . Critics! duns!
        and Fate!
Do—do your hardest—but I dine[1] at eight.
My thoughts are stolen? and my lines are halt?
Well, very likely : please to pass the salt.
Jones won't accept your bills : he funks the
        risk.
Does he? By Heavens! *potage à la bisque!*
You recollect what Titus used to say?
Did Titus dine? he *could not* lose a day.

---

[1] Qu'on me méprise, pourvu que je dine ! was the excla-
mation of one (which?) of the revolutionary sensualists of
A.D. 1789.

O dear old boy ! you ransack all the Rhine

To line your bins, then make their contents

      mine.

Who would be rich, so long as he is young

And boasts a generous but temperate tongue ?

I bring my hat, my anecdote, my laugh,

And need but kindly criticise and quaff,

Plutus repays my frequent presence here

With grasp unchanging, ever-changing cheer.

Long may the Gods preserve my palate clean

To do due justice to his deft *cuisine !*

And, O kind, compensating Time ! increase

My Banker's Balance as my youth you fleece ;

So that, a seasonable change at most,

The slender guest may smile the portly host.

And when, dear boys ! Life's Vintage slightly

      sours,

With taste discreet and temper wholly ours,

Not even Death is able to deprave,

Invert the wine-cup o'er a gourmet's grave!

Why, Life itself a dinner is indeed,

Where each contributes so that all may feed.

We all give something: some give more, some
     less;

None are excluded from the social mess:

And he who finds the bread or beverage sour,

Should send us better or should cease to lour.

I hate your churls who strut, and sulk, and
     swear

Go where they will they ever foully fare.

Believe me, friend! you 'll always find that such

Provide but little who exact so much.

Your true cosmopolite, Life's well-bred guest,

Scorns not plain dishes, though he serves the
     best;

And should there hap disaster, even dearth,

Mends the misfortune or the want with mirth.

Does not, when some rude grumbler mars the
    rout,

Instinctive justice mutter "Turn him out"?

Would we were rid of all whose gall deflowers

Their own existence and would poison ours!

    But—the clock strikes: the carriage waits: be
    trite.

Pocchini dances, Titiens sings, to-night.

Sure, you mistake?   For Lumley [k] promise
    made

Of voice not heard, limbs never yet displayed.

---

  [k] An anachronism, surely? Ah! I know too well that
we are under bondage to Smith, E. T. No more wax
candles and £1,500 worth of plate on "Her Majesty's"
stage, as in the golden gone-away days of Lumley the

Better and better: sharp's the word. The
    tier?

The first, of course—the best for eye and ear.

Gods! what a show! Right, left, the House is
    crámmed:

Our new danseuse won't, here at least, be
    damned.

What is this living, passion-prompting zone

But Venus' Cæstus once again our own?

Who prates of rainbows? By this iris bold

Prismatic hues were colourless and cold.

Magnificent. But I introduce his name for auld lang
syne's sake. Woe is all of us! Who remembers—who
can forget?—last year's representation of Oberon? Battered, bare-legged ballet-girls, and blue fire, composed the
framework of Weber's imaginative opera. Why cannot
Mr. E. T. Smith transfer his energies from Theatres to
Parliament? Judging from his scenic successes, I should
surmise that no one would so fitly represent the intelli-
gence of a Metropolitan Borough.

Above, around, below, are houris' eyes,

Flashing with quick, intelligent surprise,

And houris' blushes rapidly respond

To murmurous whispers deftly-dropped and
        fond,

Spread from the temples, eddy to the neck,

Break on the breast, and, turning at the check,

In ripples weaker rally from restraint,

Creep up the cheek and on the features faint.

Their rounded, pliant, silent-straying arms

Seem sent to guard, yet manifest their charms.

Mark how the lorgnettes cautiously they raise

Lest points, no pose so thoughtless but displays,

A too quick curiosity should hide—

For they who gaze must gazed at be beside.[1]

---

[1] "On voit une foule de petites mains, les unes prendre,
les autres demander leur lorgnettes, lesquelles montent

Now, o'er the box their beauteous busts they bend,

A foe to welcome, criticise a friend,

Unfolding or obscuring charms at will

With all the calm unconsciousness of skill,

Solving the doubt that sometimes will arise—

Whilst women wantons are, can men be wise?

Let your eyes stray from sensuous row to row

Of nude parade, and flash an honest no !

à la hauteur des yeux sans que le bras oublie la pose qu'il
doit avoir pour être gracieux ; car tandis qu'on lorgne
on peut être lorgnée, et il ne faut pas se laisser sur-
prendre."

I trust that all will appreciate my generosity, in point-
ing out what will doubtless now be called the source of
my lines—though it certainly was not—as the extract is
from "La Dame aux Perles," by Monsieur Alexandre
Dumas, fils; a book which honest folks would never
think of reading, since it would probably be condemned
to the purgatory (or hell, perhaps?) of Literature,
designated by the *National Review* as "The Lowest Deep."
Has the National Reviewer any idea that there is in
Literature "than this lowest deep a lower deep?" and
has he any suspicion what it is?

What can be Man's, whilst Woman deems *her*
    part
To bare her bosom, but to hide her heart?

  Hush! pretty prattlers!   Waving arms apart,
Æolus frees the fettered winds of Art.
Be dumb, ye dawdlers! whilst his spells con-
    found [m]
The gathered—scattered—symphonies of sound.
Cymbals barbaric clang; cowed flutes complain
As the sharp, cruel clarion cleaves the strain:
To drum deaf-bowelled, drowning sob and wail,
Scared viols shriek, that pity may prevail;
Till, with tumultuous purpose, swift and strong,
Sweeps the harmonious hurricane of Song!

------

  [m] For the benefit of literal people, I annex the primary
meaning of Confundere.; viz., to unite, mingle, combine.
—"Riddle's Lat.-Eng. Dictionary."

The curtain lifts.   Behold the " Lost One " [n]

    lain

'Mid all the woes of suitors and champagne :

Of the whole crowd the cynosure and queen,

The best-dressed woman in this sumptuous scene.

Wit—beauty—bearing—graciousness—restraint,

Gifts few possess and none can wholly feint ;

Not wife, yet woman—hurt, but not debased—

If vain, unselfish—modest, if not chaste ;

Wealth, worship, fashion, prostrate at her feet,

Yet fled with Alfred to profound retreat—

For him the World abandoned quite, again

For him endured the pantomime of men —

  " The story of "La Traviata" is too well known to require further reference than what is made to it in the Text. That the reference therein is faithful, may be tested by a glance at the Argument prefixed to the English version of the libretto, which epitomises the Lost One's history.

Her life's one chance, one yearning, straight fore-
    gone,

To save the father, sister, in the son—

Wronged, as can wrong alone a lover's skill,

For her fidelity, yet faithful still—

Doomed by disease which modifies, not mars,

Dying like light in some transparent vase—

At last in Alfred's penitent embrace,

Held to his heart and fondled to his face—

Clinging to life, but with untroubled tone

Claiming the Heaven of Virgins for her own—°

Is not this, nothing heightened, nothing glozed,

The vocal Drama but this instant closed ?

 ° In the last scene, Violetta, made acquainted with her
certain fate, exclaims in agony : "Great God! to die so
young !"   But, submitting to the inevitable, she gives
Alfred a portrait of herself, for the benefit of some future
wife, whom he is to tell "that she who gave it thee, 'midst
the Saints in Heaven, prays for her and thee."

Hark! how fresh plaudits plaudits fresh repeat,

And purest posies kiss the "Lost One's"
     feet!

Do I complain our maidens should acquire

Her story? Ah! I nought could *more* desire

Than they should know, and, knowing, would
     reclaim

At once their sex, their sisters, and their
     shame.

But by what moral or dramatic laws

Bare you the consequence, but veil the cause?

Vicious results prompt vice, beheld alone:

Let all be hidden or let all be known.

The henbane's flower poisons whom it lures;

Pluck you but deeper, 'tis the root that cures.

Whom noble still in infamy we saw,

In frailty faithful, fair despite her flaw,

Why was this woman with the world at
     strife,

Nor maid revered, nor consecrated wife?

Why the song silent on the only part

Of her career that might instruct the heart,

But that the story of her *early* years

Were sure to stir (beyond those surface tears

Which straightway dry beneath to-morrow's
     drought)

A fertile pity and an active thought?

And thus the partial Drama you applaud

Is a mere flaunting falsity and fraud.

What is the spell that 'twixt a saint and sinner

The diff'rence makes? a sermon? bah! a dinner.

The odds and ends our silken Claras waste

Would keep our calico Clarissas chaste.

Celia! the lace from off your parasol

Had held Celinda's sunburnt virtue whole:

A hundred pounds would coy have made the
nude,

A thousand pounds the prostitute a prude,

And little more expenditure of pelf

Fanny a bigot bitter as yourself!

Hence! surpliced sophists! who with fasts and
cries

Would fain compel Omniscience to be wise!

What if, instead of craving drought or rain,

You built a reservoir or delved a drain?

Instead of prayers and platitudes demure,

Diffused the wealth that keeps peers' daughters
pure?

With scorn the stalwart pauper's prayers you
spurn,

Yet whine to God for wage yourselves might
earn.

There is nor tempest, torrent, drouth, nor
      wind,

Which is not big with blessings to mankind ;

And each fomenting passion in the breast

Might add to life a sparkle and a zest:

Yet those you let devastate and deflower,

And these but make existence flat and sour !

Blaspheming fools ! with shrieks the skies you
      rend

Against the very benefits they send ;

And howl to God, Who meant you for
      divine,

For grace to sink your species into swine !

This earth is man's : not God's, *except* as
      man's :

And man's the action in it that He plans.

True to his scheme, He never intervenes:

The end being human, human are the means.

What is man's end?   To know and to be free.[p]

Think you to compass it by tracts and tea?

Labonr[q] is prayer—the only prayer that serves—

And all beside it but disordered nerves.

Your God, you point to, paused not till He could

Feel His work done, and see that it was good.

Then did He rest.   Your work done, so may

     you:

But "days of rest," whilst work remains to do!

The hungry feed: dismiss the thirsty slaked:

Take you the stranger in, and clothe the naked:

Visit the sick, the prison-house, the slum;

And then, "ye blessed of my Father, come!"[r]

---

[p] "You shall know the truth, and the truth shall make you free."—*St. Paul.*

[q] Qui laborat, orat: is one of the oldest aphorisms of the Catholic Church.

[r] "Then shall the King say to them that shall be on his

Oh ! when shall Toil assert its proper price,

At once prayer, fasting, alms, and sacrifice ?

And Men the workers proffer, as they plod,

A jubilation and a hymn to God ?

Truce to this moral thunder : for advance

Fleet-footed laurelled Daphnes[3] of the Dance.

What first but vaguely Opera designs,

The Ballet next developes and defines :

The sentimental to the sensuous grows,

And pointless trilling into pointed toes.

---

right hand : Come, ye blessed of my Father, possess the
kingdom prepared for you from the foundation of the
world.

"For I was hungry, and you gave me to eat : I was
thirsty, and you gave me to drink : I was a stranger, and
you took me in.

"Naked, and you clothed me : sick, and you visited
me : I was in prison, and you came unto me."—*Matt.* xxv.
34—36.

[3] *Daphne*, a maiden loved and pursued by Apollo ; and

Now wake the fathers who securely slept

Whilst Alfred wooed and Violetta wept,

Rub up their spectacles and strain their gaze

At bounding Zina dressed in shoes and

    stays:

Now love-struck boys transfer their fickle eyes

From Mary's trinkets to Morlacchi's thighs;

Whilst mothers, sisters, sweethearts, wives, ap-

    plaud

The tight proportions of a twirling bawd.

Must we then stop it? no: unleash the Town

To hunt a Nicholson or Warton down;[t]

---

when overtaken by the erotic Song-god, tantalisingly
transformed into a laurel. The legend does not say if it
was a prickly one: but we may presume it was.

[t] *Nicholson ... Warton.* Caterers for the taste of what
my hair-dresser calls "the lower orders of people what
exist." The owners of Walhallas, Rainbow Nymphs,
Days of Rhodes Revived, &c.

The scent will take, the Cider Cellars close,

And Haddo,[u] hoodwinked, not insist on hose.

Thus, with the prudent chastity of clique,

Protect the Ballet 'gainst the Poses Plastiques.

Whilst we, surveying this decorous stage,

Admire the pastimes of a modest age,

An errant curiosity inquires

Whither the Drama, England's boast, retires.

Let bounding profligates their limbs display

Where "further off"[x] chaste Hermia's lover "lay."

---

[u] Lord Haddo, now Earl of Aberdeen, has made violent efforts in the House of Commons to put a stop to the use of nude models in Schools of Art. I hope that I do not wrong his lordship in concluding that he extends his moral indignation to the nude, when exhibited before a larger and more public assemblage.

[x] SCENE—*A wood near Athens.*

Hermia.—But, gentle friend, for love and courtesy
LIE FURTHER OFF; in human modesty

Let figurante trip where Siddons stepped,

And jugglers[y] grin where once Macready wept ;

Yet High Art surely somewhere makes a stand.

Somewhere !   Well, where ? in Wych Street or

    the Strand ?

Is it where saucy Wilton[z] winks her way,

And says the more the less she has to say ?

Such separation, as may well be said
Becomes a virtuous bachelor and a maid,
So far be distant ; and good night, sweet friend ;
Thy love ne'er alter till thy sweet life end.
    Lysander.—Amen, amen, to that fair prayer, say I ;
And then end life, when I end loyalty.
                (They sleep.)
        Midsummer's Night's Dream.

[y] By "Jugglers," I do not refer to the Administrative Reformers, who also performed at Drury Lane Theatre, but to the Chinese ditto, who delighted crowded houses by innocuously flinging knives at each others' heads.

[z] Miss Marie Wilton is every way charming, and can act only in those parts which are written for her ; and it is no fault—but rather talent—of hers, that she creates a

Is it where Robson,[a] servile to the Town,

Discards the Actor and adopts the Clown ?

Where Toole or Compton, perfect in his part,

Touches each sense except the head and heart ?

Where mobs " recal " the wit of Rogers' wig,

Applaud a pun and recompense a jig ?

Seek where you will, you still will fail to find

More than a grinning, mountebank mankind.

Conscious of paltry purpose or of none,

No pride in winning, peace in having won ;

Craving a respite from pursuit of pelf,

Our age in shows seeks shelter from itself.[b]

------

more lively sensation when she is not speaking than when she is.

[a] The great—the only—*tragic* actor we have : who, as Mazeppa, lies in tights on a bare-backed steed stuffed with straw, and requests a hungry vulture of the same material to " keep up his pecker."

[b] Il faut des spectacles dans les grandes villes, et des romans aux peuples corrompus.— *Jean Jacques Rousseau.*

It strains at mirth, but like abandoned Boy

Debauched by sports that shatter whom they cloy,

Has lost its healthy appetite for joy:

And yet too slothful to arise and scan

The splendid toils allotted to the Man,

Toys with remorse, and as it supine lies,

" O give me back my youth ! " unblushing cries.

Put out the lights: rub off the paint: the Play,

Sir, is performed; your carriage stops the way.

Well then, good night: the morn will soon be up:

You go to slumber? No! I go to sup.

Bah ! I forgot. First Hansom ! double fare !

Drive fast as Fate to 50, Belgrave Square.[c]

---

[c] One of my (I have mauy) literal friends comes and asks me, " Why 50, Belgrave Square?" And when I answer, "Because there are only *forty-nine* numbers," he goes away, offended at my rudeness.

Botanic Shows, where crowds and tactics
    tear
Too yielding daughters from a mother's chair :
Water excursions, when full boats divide
Some pretty novice from a sister's side ;
Or garden-fêtes, when, after absence spent—
The whole time, really, in the public tent—
An anxious niece a careless aunt pursues,
Conscious of wrong, so ready to accuse :
To these be honour ; but the Ball—the Ball—
Combines, continues, and excels them all.
Here, with complacency, strict matrons see
Maids and Moss-troopers[d] polking, knee to knee.
Their kindly gaze examines and exalts
The closer contact of the chaster waltz.

---

[d] "Free Lances" is a recognized pseudonym. Surely,
" Moss-troopers" rings more like home coinage.

Look where they smile, the grey-haired guardians
    set

To scout decorum, sanction etiquette.^e

Louder, ye viols! shrilly, cornets! blow!

Who is this prophet that denounces woe?

---

^e I find by my "Spectator," that matters were not much better a hundred and fifty years ago; for on the 17th day of May, A.D. 1711, the following complaint is laid before him by one who says that he "is not yet old enough to be a fool."

"I was amazed to see my girl handled by and handling young fellows with so much familiarity; and I could not have thought it had been in the child. They very often made use of a most impudent and lascivious step, called ' setting,' which I know not how to describe to you, but by telling you that it is the very reverse of 'back to back.' At last an impudent young dog bid the fiddlers play a dance called ' Moll Pately,' and after having made two or three capers, ran to his partner, locked his arms in hers, and whisked her round cleverly above ground in such a manner, that I, who sat upon one of the lowest benches, saw further above her shoe than I could think fit to acquaint you with. I could no longer endure these enormities; wherefore, just as my girl was going to be made a whirligig, I ran in, seized on the child, and carried her home."

Whirl fast! whirl long! ye gallants and ye
    girls!
Cling closer still; dance down these cursëd
    churls.
Be crowned, ye fair! with poppies, newly-
    blown,
Fling loose your tresses, and relax your zone!
From floating gauze let dreamy perfumes rise,
Infuse a fiercer fervour in your eyes!
Whirl faster, closer, until passion's drouth
Play in the tell-tale muscles of the mouth,
The furious Circle bid a truce to masks,
And Nature answer all that Nature asks!

  Bless us and save us!   What tirade is this?
My choleric friend! is anything amiss?
This scene, your anti-sensual strictures doom,
Is not an Orgy, but——an auction-room.

These panting damsels, dancing for their lives,

Are only maidens waltzing into wives.

Those smiling matrons are appraisers sly

Who regulate the dance, the squeeze, the
    sigh,

And each base cheapening buyer having chid,

Knock down their daughters to the noblest bid.

  An honest time there was, when girl and
    boy

Might love and yet not jeopardise their joy :

When, in faint laughs were fainter whispers
    drowned,

Yet was no ill suspected in the sound.

'Chance, did they stray to sit and smile apart,

No frowns arraigned their vagrancy of heart :

Unfettered but unforced, instinctive Youth

Erred into right, and trembled into truth.

No jealous frames, no artificial fires,

Stunted their growth, but hurried their desires.

Their graceful fondness gradually grew,

By drouth of absence, by reunion's dew;

Cheered by the sun, or saddened by the
   shower,

On each it throve, and fretted into flower.

Not e'en a parent prematurely pressed

The yet young secret from a basking breast;

Ripened by outer warmth, by inner sap,

It fell, spontaneous, in a mother's lap.

"You do not blame us, mother? will not
   part?

'Tis not to-day I give him up my heart:

He stepped across its threshold long before,

And is its household god for evermore."

Could he scarce yet sustain a husband's charge,

(His fortune narrow, though his love was large)

He was not exiled by a venal Fate:

A boy might work, a maiden sure might wait.

Love mingled with the grave concerns of Life,

Tempered the toil and sanctified the strife:

No danger difficult, no hardship hard,

Risked for the promise of that rich reward.

It made his dullest drudgery divine,

That brave resolve, "my darling shall be mine!"

While she could feel she helped him in his part,

Strengthened his purpose, purified his heart.

Till, aims accomplished, youth's brisk battle
    won,

They rushed together, mystic Two-in-One.

How is it now? Morality's advance

Demands for Love the strictest surveillance.

We banish with the glare of vulgar eyes

The lights and shadows of Love's coy disguise:

Rude ears invade—(Propriety insists)—

Her would-be secret, solitary lists;

Spoil all her tender tournay; put to rout

Those skilful skirmishers the heart sends out

In boldly-cautious converse, to make known

Another's weakness, but to screen its own:

No sweet lane-loiterings, no twilight strolls,

Induce the gradual intercourse of souls.

Two Balls—three Dinners—one Botanic Fête—

" You mean to try the matrimonial state?

Sir! your intentions? Marry, or depart;

You   must   not   trifle   with   my   daughter's
            heart."

" I did intend, but—truth to tell—as yet

My means are—" " Hold! you mean you are
            in debt.

You're much mistaken, let me tell you, sir !

If you conceive you'll ever marry *her*."

He goes: consoles himself as best he can:

And she? she marries money and a man.

A female and no fortune—it is just;

So nought is left of Love except its lust.

All Love is lust, but Love is something more:

Each girl 's at heart a woman or a whore.

Hard words? hard laws. The words have been

    revised:

There are some sores which must be cauterized.'

  Just as unskilled equestrians restrain

All healthful action, but give vice the rein,

So do these social laws unwisely err,

They check the angel but the demon spur,

' I am haunted by the belief that Voltaire has somewhere said the same thing. However, it is so true, that
it is worth saying again; especially to people to whom
Voltaire is more or less a sealed writer.

Making e'en kindly courtesies a curse,

Manners no better and our morals worse.

    You knew Blanche Darley? could we but once
        more

Behold that belle and pet of '54!

Not e'en a whisper, vagrant up to Town

From hunt or race-ball, augured her renown.

Far in the wolds sequestered life she led,

Fair and unfettered as the fawn she fed :

Caressed the calves, coquetted with the colts,

Bestowed much tenderness on turkey poults,

Bullied the huge ungainly bloodhound pup,

Tiffed with the terrier, coaxed to make it up :

The farmers quizzed about the ruined crops,

The fall of barley, and the rise of hops :

Gave their wives counsel, but gave flannel too,

Present where'er was timely deed to do;

Known, loved, applauded, prayed for far and wide—
The wandering sunshine of the country side.
So soft her tread, no nautilus that skims
With sail more silent than her liquid limbs.
Her hair so golden that, did slanting eve
With a stray curl its sunlight interweave,
Smit with surprise, you gazed but could not guess
Which the warm sunbeam, which the warmer
   tress.
Her presence was low music : when she went,
She left behind a dreamy discontent,
As sad as silence when a song is spent.

She came—we saw—were conquered : one and
  all,
We donned the fetters of delicious thrall ;
We fetched, we carried, dawdled, doffed, and did,
Just as our Blanche the beautiful would bid.

Such crowds petitioned her at every ball

For "just one waltz," she scarce could dance
      at all!

Besieged her card with such intrigues and
      sighs,

It might have been the pass-book to the skies.

We lost our heads.   Have women wiser grown?

A marvel surely, had she kept her own.

  But brief our madness.   Had we heard the
      news?

Vaux has proposed.   Vaux! reeking from the
      stews;

That remnant, Vaux! shrunk, tottering, palsied,
      wan!

An Earl by right, by courtesy a man.

That soldier-sycophant, with seam and scar

Gashed deep, but not in battle's joyful jar!

He with the cannon's never blent his breath,

Nor gaily galloped up the gaps of death :

Too rich to roam, in bloodless fields and fights

A lie at Brooks's, black-ball drops at White's.

Senilely supple if you lure or warn,

Now prowls the Quadrant, now confers with
      Kahn.

   Romantic boys ! be still. Will angry names

Like "battered beast" annul an Earldom's
      claims?

Life is not wholly sentiment and stars :

Venus wed Mercury as well as Mars.

Hush your lewd tattle ! seek your slighted
      beds !

A cornet waltzes, but a colonel weds.

The Countess comes. Before her marriage vow,

Only men praised her : women praise her now.

See what avail a carriage and a pair!

You lose a lover, but—you gain a stare.

The world, to kindly compensation prone,

Gives you its honour when you lose your own.

Corrupt in heart, in head-dress if correct,

Our well-bred race rewards you with respect.

Who more respected than my Lady Vaux?

The Town collects and wonders as she walks.

What if the Earl be absent from her side,

Whilst others near it—gouty Earls must ride.

Let those, whose line but yesterday began,

Crave for the coarse capacities of man;

Vaux gave his wealth, his peerage, Blanche her
       face—

Your vulgar wants invade not Chesham Place.

Is it so sad to have one's husband old?

The mother's milk but mars the maiden's
       mould;

And Blanche, whilst fruitful spouses fade so
    fast,

Shall bear her barren beauty to the last !

What ! . . So they say . . Bah ! Nonsense . .
    But it's true :

True, sure enough—will lay you ten to two.

Jack saw the brief, Respondent's name en-
    dorsed. . . .

Great God in heaven ! Blanche to be divorced !

O scalding shame ! that name, last season's
    toast,

Is never mentioned, or is mourned at most ;

Save where lewd lawyers, on their benches
    perched,

In joke obscene send round the name that's
    smirched ;

Or, fouler still, amidst lascivious roar,

The Coal Hole[g] travesties one trial more !

.

    But what of Frank? to whom she early
        gave

Her love, that guardian-angel sent to save :

To whose kind counsels would we list alone,

We ne'er should dash our foot against a stone.

A truer, braver bosom never throbbed

Than that poor boy's, whom fashion foully robbed.

In camps begot, his earliest desire

Turned to the sabre of his slaughtered sire.

But Peace, oppressive Peace becalmed the world :

Fluttered no pennon, not a wave was curled.

---

   [g] In the " Coal-Hole" is or was held, a mimic Court of Law, under the Presidency of Baron Nicholson, with the avowed occupation of parodying celebrated Matrimonial Causes.

When would War's lances tear the welkin
    dun?
When battle's bugles summon up the sun?
The barrack life in stagnant country town,
The bootless charge o'er undefended down,
He chafed at all—court-martial, march, parade,
And almost cursed the choice himself had
    made.

    He met with Blanche. Complaint began to
    cease:
Who knows? Her smile might compensate for
    Peace.
He was too poor to prate as one that woos,
But not—who is?—too poor to love and lose.
That devil Circumstance, who smooths the way
To those who "may not," blocks to those who
    "may,"

Threw them together : wheresoe'er they went,

They met as though by purposed accident.

A pettish parting by a wicker gate

Unsealed their secret, but to seal their fate.

He called her back : she turned on him her
　　　eyes

With a most swift significant surprise,

Gazed straight into his soul, that moment bare,

And saw her own bright image trembling there;

But in that gaze unmasked she to his view

Eyes that, though piercing his, reflected too !

　Did they not part?　Ah ! lips, which once have
　　　kissed,

Are impotent to reason or resist.

Who ne'er was tempted knows not how to
　　　teach,

And he who falls will soon forget to preach.

The Scribe may scowl, the Pharisee may chide—
But Human Nature 's always Justified.

Did they not part ?   When Europe's wild alarms
Tore him from hers to Conflict's sterner arms,
And proud fair England gave her boys to guard
From Tartar maw what Turkish lust hath marred,
Joyful he went : ere long he would return
Whom most would sigh for, none besought would
    spurn.
The foe-fleshed hand, the decorated brow
Might seize the spoil they dared not sue for,
    now.

In the Light Charge the gallant won his spurs,
And prized his laurels, since his laurels hers.
Now might he write, and with unchallenged claim
Fling at her feet the fulness of his fame.

E

I saw that bright broad face shrink cold and hard:
Blanche Darley's answer ?—Lady Vaux's card !

A first babe draining a young mother's breast,
A kneeling Catholic maiden just confessed,
Are not more pure, more welcome to the
      wise,
Than hapless Love in Courtesy's disguise.

How courteous he ! A smile, a look, from
      Blanche
Swayed him as breeze a young lithe willow
      branch.
Yet none could guess, save only those who knew,
What flogged-down fondness whined and crouched
      from view.
No longer love, but worship, warped his mind ;
He held her holy—worship made him blind.

He did not see, what others saw and scanned,

A rich prize ready for the boldest hand.

Or seeing, spared the Fruit of Good-and-Ill,

With *Her* to dwell within his Eden still;

Perchance   not   jealous   now   that   man   and
        wife,

Plucking, had proved the nakedness of life.

Oh, what a dawn, when first he waked to own

He walked his fond Fool's Paradise—alone!

He who, despite his sorely baffled aim,

Survived his loss, could not survive her shame.

In that vast Empire fastened-on by fraud,

And since by clanking sabres overawed,

Rebellion brake like storm-clouds in the night!

He asked a sword, and hurried to the fight;

Rang out the war-cry with his Spartan wont—

" Cravens to rear! rough-riders to the front ! "

Stern to the last, stemmed triumph's torrent tide ;
And if unconquering, unconquered died.

But Blanche?   Oh! surely the unblemished
    snow
Was not——Hush ! Hush ! Enough for you to
    know
That she, who once such curt refusal gave
To share Frank's bed, would gladly share his
    grave.

Darkness retreats, its misty banners furled ;
The Sun's couched lances scour along the world.
Skulk to your beds, ye Bacchanals of Night !
The Day stalks in and stares upon your rite.
On wine-stains, crumpled wreaths, and clammy
    lips,
And eyes bedimmed with surfeit's foul eclipse,

On cheeks where roses blown have ceased to
    smile,

Or stay to show how false they were the while,

On slattern hair, whose short thin wisps make
    known

How much of former fulness was its own,

On broken fans and irritated corns,

Brows steeped in sweat that earns not nor
    adorns:

Away! away! let sleep—such sleep as hies

To Fashion's fagged yet feverish votaries—

With lurements fresh to-morrow's limbs invest,

And friendly paint and padding do the rest.[h]

---

[h] Written with whatever dissimilar meaning, the lines
of Ovid upon Echo may, without strain, be applied to the
disordered figures of three o'clock in the morning.

> Et neque jam color est misto candore rubori;
> Nec vigor, et vires, et quæ modo visa placebant;
> *Nec corpus remanet.*

Why further follow, flogging Fashion's faults?
The Muse will flag, but Folly never halts.
Write as I will, the prurience of men
Invents new vice, to paralyze my pen.
From class to class the mummery descends:
I seek in vain for contrast or for friends.
All ranks to equal turpitude aspire;
Those make the mode, these mimic in the mire.
See salon morals vagrant on the flags,
Vice's torn tawdry shown as Virtue's rags,
Pure, simple Woman, brazen, scented, curled,
And God-like Man, the clothes-horse of the
       world!

Who think by verse to better make the bad,
I grant it freely, must be vain or mad.
From Horace downwards, monitory rhymes
Have but amused, and mended not the times.

Yet in an Age when each one strives to hide

The scorn he feels for every one beside,

I claim the precious privilege of youth,

Never to speak except to speak the truth.

Urge you that youth should ne'er presume to
    scold,

Since Satire suits the wise alone, and old,

Ah! age is not invariably nice,

And wisdom oft grows lenient to vice.

Besides: much more impartially the boy

May scowl at sports himself could yet enjoy.

Perforce should impotent repentant rake

Denounce the havoc he no more can make,

Dyspeptic pauper against feasts protest

His purse can't reach, his stomach can't
    digest,

Or paralytic moralists condemn

The lips that now no longer lust for *them*,

Would you not say the fable of the grapes

Fitted these censors in their sober shapes?

Not rich nor beggared, blasé nor a child,

Not quite unblemished, yet not quite defiled,

Neither too old to want, too young to win,

Acquainted but not surfeited with sin,

A guest sometimes where meats and wines abound,

And yet, thank God! my head and stomach
     sound,

Rich human blood redundant in my veins,

And Beauty's bounties my most grateful gains,

By none befooled, I abdicate my age

To lash the pastimes which my peers engage.

  Let purists frowning at my verse pretend

To mourn the means and not to see the end,

Deny the sore, so deprecate the knife—

But as our ballet, so our social life.

Whilst quite enough is deftly bared to sight

To lend to lust a lecherous delight,

As deftly too is just so much obscure

As makes the good (but timid) half endure.

Strip off this insincerity of gauze

Which baulks the hiss and sanctions the ap-
plause.

Perchance—and thither is my satire aimed—

When *all* is naked, *some* will feel ashamed.

Welcome release! The Season gasps and
dies,

And Fashion's Crowd to seaside quarters flies.

What though the Tide's uncompromising roar

Thunders its truths, terrific, on the shore,

Deaf to its voice, they only there prolong

The kill-time shifts recorded in my song.

Not them I follow : but that dear old beach,
Will I seek out, where far beyond the reach
Of flirts and flippants, will the faithful foam
Fawn at my feet and gambol round my home.
Vagrant, I surely shall the lesson learn,
To prize results, but recompense to spurn ;
Since every breaker, how supreme soe'er
The wealth its individual bosom bear,
Impelled by no poor egotist desires,
To the community of waves retires
Wholly as undistinguished as before,
When it has cast its corals on the shore.

THE END.

ROBERT HARDWICKE, PRINTER, 192, PICCADILLY.